ROBERT G.

Zoey Zimmerman and the Zombie Pigeon

Copyright © 2011 by Robert C. Mason

First Edition

Chapter 1

Zoey tugged at her sleeve using it to wipe the sweat from her forehead. Un-slinging her back pack she removed two bottles, passing one bottle to Tanner, "Water?"

Tanner took the bottle, unscrewed the cap and took a big gulp, "Thanks. Can we take a break now?"

Zoey glanced down at her watch then up at the blistering Arizona sun, "Yeah, we've been walking for almost two hours. How about that big rock under that Palo Verde tree over there?"

Tanner turned and wearily made his way over to the shady spot Zoey pointed out. Sitting down he let out an exhausted, "Finally."

Zoey sat beside Tanner, jabbing an elbow in his side, "Oh come on you wimp. You and the guys will shoot hoops for hours in this heat without a break. Why is this so much worse then that?"

"Basketball is fun," he replied taking a drink from his water bottle again, "Where's the fun in walking up and down a mountain, especially when it is a hundred-twenty degrees?"

Zoey rolled her eyes, "Oh pah-leeze, it can't be more then a hundred and fifteen out."

Tanner laughed shooting water out of his nose, "Ow!"

Laughing, Zoey took the water bottle back from Tanner, "Gimmie that before you hurt yourself some more."

"I'm sorry Zo, but we've been out here for two hours and not one sign of this bird anywhere. In fact, we've hardly seen any animals out here at all. It's too hot out. Even the desert animals know enough to keep out of this heat."

Zoey looked around and knew that he was right. They had hardly seen any wildlife today, "I know Tank, but that's even more reason for us to keep looking. If it's too hot for the animals that live out here to be out how long do you think a pet cockatoo will last?"

"I know Zo, but…"

Zoey pulled a piece of paper out of her back pack and put it in Tanner's hand.

"Oh don't show me the flyer again."

"Just look at that picture Tank."

Tanner pulled his ball cap down over his eyes and shook his head, "I don't wanna."

Zoey pinched a big chunk of his side and twisted a bit, "Look at it."

"Alright alright," he shouted in a combination of laughter and pain, "You win."

He adjusted his hat then rubbed his side after she let him go and looked over the flyer again, consciously avoiding the photo at the top of the page.

LOST PET
6 MONTH OLD COCKATOO
FAMILY DISTRAUGHT
REWARD
(602) 555-1138
WE MISS YOU CALLIOPE

Zoey pointed to the photo of Calliope on the flyer, "Look at that face Tank, she's just a baby."

Just like Zoey, Tanner loved animals and they both knew it. It was one of the things that brought them together and made them best friends. It was also one of the things that she could always use to keep him tagging along on these kinds of expeditions.

While Tanner didn't possess Zoeys' gift with animals, being friends with her gave him a level of appreciation for animals that not many people had. It also made it very hard to say "No" to Zoey Zimmerman.

Zoey pulled a lunch box out of her back pack, "Hot pocket?"

Tanner raised an eyebrow, tilted his head and looked her way, "You are evil."

Zoey laughed, "You look just like Alton when you tilt your head like that."

"So now I look like a beagle?"

"No silly," she giggled. "Pepperoni or broccoli and cheese?" She asked already knowing what the answer would be.

"Pepperoni please."

"I don't mean you look like a dog," she said handing him a foiled wrapped Hot Pocket, "I mean you tilt your head the same way Alton does when he try's to be cute."

Tanner pulled back the foil and took a big bite, "So I look *and* act like a dog?"

"Well, in this heat you do sort of smell like a dog."

"Hey, it's hot out here, and I'm sure you don't smell like roses right now either."

"Stop it you dork, I'm only teasing. And don't talk with your mouth full. It's gross."

Tanner covered his mouth and swallowed, "Seriously though Zo, we've covered a lot of the park and we haven't got much to go on. We need some new info."

"You're right. Let me put in a call to the local scouts."

Zoey stood pulled off a few pinches of crust from the end of her Hot Pocket and spread the crumbs out around the trail a few feet away from the shade of their resting place and then returned to the cool shade of the tree.

"How long do you think that will take?" Tanner asked polishing off the last of his lunch.

"Maybe twenty or thirty minutes. Probably less if you had chipped in with some of yours."

"Sorry, but you know I don't mess around when it comes to Hot Pockets."

Zoey shook her head in amusement, returning her lunch box to her backpack. Crossing her legs in her lap she waited.

Pulling his ball cap down over his eyes Tanner laid back on the rock. It was too hot for him to fall asleep, but at least it was a break from the walking. He knew the drill when Zoey was reaching out for "scouts" as she liked to call them. '*Sit still and be quiet*' was rule number one.

He wasn't really sure how much time had gone before he heard Zoey's voice.

"Hello there. I was wondering if you could please help me out."

Tanner heard birds chirping and he tried to imagine what was being said on the other end of the conversation.

"Yes, I am speaking to you. My name is Zoey, I was wondering if I could ask your help."

A smile slowly crept across Tanner's face. It was always like this at first.

"Yes, I can understand everything your saying, and that's not a polite way to refer to humans. It is a terrible generalization."

I bet one of them called her a planet wrecker Tanner thought to himself.

"Yes, it is quite unusual. I do get that a lot."

Tanner laughed, knocking his hat off his face and onto the ground beside him.

"No wait. It's okay, he's with me," Zoey said turning her head to glare at Tanner, "Say hi Tanner."

Tanner silently mouthed the word "Sorry" as he slowly sat up, remembering rule number two, '*Sudden movements are scary.*' He paused briefly before standing and slowly made his way over to where Zoey was kneeling on the trail and knelt down just a little bit behind her on her left.

Sitting across from them he recognized a pair of Gambel's Quail, extremely common for the South Mountain Park area of south Phoenix. The gray and brown body colorings of the male and female quail were nearly identical, except for the black face and copper colored head of the male. Both quail possessed the distinct head plume that the species is known for.

"Hi there."

The plumes atop the head of both quail bounced as they looked back and forth in shock from each other to Zoey and Tanner and back.

"No, unfortunately he can't, just me."

Tanner pointed his thumb at Zoey, "She's the brains, I'm just the muscle."

Their plumes bounced just as Tanner thought they might when a quail laughed.

"That's not true," Zoey insisted, "We work as a team. We specialize in finding lost pets and returning them to their Caretakers."

According to Zoey, Caretaker is the preferred term over Pet Owner by animals. Since pets do have free will they don't like to be considered property "owned" by anyone. Some animals enjoy having a Caretaker, some don't, and the ones that don't are the ones that run away.

The female quail chirped loudly causing her plume to bounce quickly making Tanner wondered if that was what a quail looked like when it was angry and yelling.

"Well yes I know, having a Caretaker is not for everyone, but some animals find it enjoyable."

The quail chirped again, softer this time.

"No, of course not. We would never force an animal back to a Caretaker if they did not want to be taken back."

Zoey was always very respectful of an animals wish to either return or not return to a Caretaker. Forcing a pet back to a home it did not want to be was not an option as far as she was concerned. Some Caretakers took wonderful care of their pets, and some didn't and there was no way she would return a pet back to a bad home.

Plumes on both birds bounced as they spoke to each other before turning back to Zoey.
"Thank you," Zoey replied producing the lost pet flyer for the couple to view, "We are looking for a lost baby cockatoo. Have you seen her around the preserve?"

The quail couple moved closer to the teens to get a better look at the photo.

The male quail appeared to get quite excited as he starting hopping up and down flapping his wings, which of course made his plume bounce quite comically.

"You have?" Zoey exclaimed, "Where? How long ago?"

The male continued his bouncing and flapping, his plume bouncing wildly the whole time.

Comprehension between Zoey and a new animal sometimes took some time. Animals, especially wild animals, didn't always have the same words to describe things that humans used so it sometimes took a while for Zoey to figure out what was being described.

While he watched Tanner thought back to early on in their friendship to the first time Zoey tried to explain to him what it was like to communicate with animals. Domestic animals she explained, especially pets that were around humans all the time, where very easy to understand. They picked up human words from exposure just like a person does growing from infancy to adulthood.

Zoey was not even able to explain how she is able to understand the chirps, squeaks, growls and other noises that make up animal communication. She just can.

The how never mattered to Tanner. He was content enough knowing she talked to them, they understood her and she understood them. The exact definition of how it all happened was irrelevant to him.

"Oh, do you mean a gazebo? Like this?" Zoey drew a picture in the sand with her finger.

Tanner snickered as the bird nodded, causing his plume to bop him in the face several times.

"The gazebo by the petroglyphs? Thank you so very much," Zoey crushed a couple of saltine crackers she took out of a baggie in her back pack and sprinkled them on the trail.

After a few chirps the birds quickly began dining on the freshly crumbled crackers as the teens stood and dusted themselves off.

"How long ago did they see her?" Tanner asked.

"It's hard to say. They don't really use time other then sun up and sun down, but they said it was not long before they ran into us."

Unfolding the preserve trail map Tanner estimated their location, "That gazebo is about a mile north from where we are right now."

Zoey pulled her back pack on, "Okay let's get moving."

***

Fifteen minutes later the gazebo came into view, "Keep your eyes peeled."

"Yep. So what did they call you?" Tanner asked.

"Who?"

"Those quail. You told them it wasn't polite to refer to humans that way. What did they call you?"

"You know I don't like to foster hate between people and critters."

"Aw c'mon. You know I don't take it personal."

"They called me a crazy bi-ped," Zoey said through grinded teeth.

"Ha hah, I had guessed planet wrecker, but I like crazy bi-ped."

"That's not funny," she replied socking him in the arm. "Now start calling Calliope and let me see if I can hear her answer back."

Zoey stood motionless, closed her eyes and starting breathing deep and slowly. Tanner knew she was all business now.

"I hope I am saying this right. Ca-lie-oh-pee! Ca-lie-oh-pee, c'mere girl!"

Tanner waited.

"Again please."

"Ca-lie-oh-pee!"

"I hear her! Ask her where she is."

Tanner pumped his fist, "Yes! Where are you girl?"

Tanner knew they were almost home free now that Zoey could hear Calliope. It was just a matter of pin pointing where she was at.

"She says she is in the roof of the house. I am guessing the gazebo, come on."

The pair sped off towards the gazebo and let out a collective sigh of relief when sure enough they found one very scared cockatoo hiding up in the rafters of the gazebo.

"Hi Calliope, my name is Zoey and this is Tanner. We're here to take you back to your Caretakers. They miss you."

Calliope hesitantly backed up and squawked.

"Yes, dogs can be quite scary when they bark. It's quite understandable for you to fly out an open door like that when you're scared."

Calliope squawked again.

"No they're not angry, they're worried about you."

Tanner held up the flyer, "See? It says right here, 'We miss you Calliope.' They have pictures of you all over."

Zoey held out her arm to provide her with a roost, "I know you're scared. I promise we won't hurt you. Come on down."

After a brief hesitation Calliope swooped down and landed on Zoey's arm, "Good girl."

"Shall I make the call Zo?"

"Sure, tell your mom we'll be waiting for her at the Visitor center."

Tanner pulled out his cell phone and pressed the speed dial for his mom, "Another mission accomplished."

Chapter 2

Major Lee swiped his identification card thru the card reader changing the light above the laboratory door from red to green. The immense metal door slid open allowing General Lucas and his entourage access into the most heavily guarded, top secret lab at FutureCore Industries.

Hearing the alarm, marking the opening of the door, Dr. Cosby looked up from his desk to see the General enter his lab. Even without the company of half a dozen soldiers General Lucas was an imposing figure, standing at nearly six foot five and a muscular frame the General commanded respect wherever he went.

General Lucas was the top liaison for the United States Joint Chiefs of Staff and the numerous corporations and research companies that contracted with the US Military on countless types of projects. It was the Generals' job to ensure that the money the government was spending was being used properly and that labs that were not producing results were shut down. This made the General a very powerful and important man, physical stature not withstanding.

Dr. Cosby on the other hand was far less then intimidating. A short chubby balding man he was often the subject of ridicule among his peers, even within the company he helped found, FutureCore. While Dr. Cosby viewed himself as completely devoted to his work others referred to him as an obsessive personality-less workaholic. Coupled with his gruff personality, once described to him by a college professor as "the complete absence of a filter when speaking," Dr. Cosby more often then not worked alone. He usually said what was on his mind, oblivious to how his words could, and often did, hurt others.

Dr. Cosby knew the General did not personally visit labs very often himself unless that lab was on the list for contract renewal or one step away from losing its contract for lack of productivity. The largest companies had a member of the Generals' staff on site for monitoring and reporting. As the largest military contractor in Arizona, FutureCore had an assigned liaison from the Generals staff.

Dr. Cosby and the other researchers meet with that liaison Major Lee weekly to keep him updated on their various projects.

Knowing that FutureCores' contract was not up for renewal review for another thirteen months Dr. Cosby easily surmised that the Generals' visit was not going to be an enjoyable one for him or FutureCore.

Rising from his desk the doctor greeted his high ranking guest, "General Lucas, to what do I owe the pleasure?"

Ignoring the doctors' offer of a handshake the General looked around surveying the lab, "You can dispense with the pleasantries doctor. Major Lee informs me that you haven't given him a new progress report for each of the last four weeks."

"Well yes General, but…"

"Considering the fact that funding for your project alone represents over $100,000 a week of FutureCores' contract you have provided us with nothing for nearly half a million dollars the last month. If you can't show me something today then by this time tomorrow your contract will be nothing more then a memory."

The doctor heart skipped a beat at the idea of losing his funding. His research on the human immune system had made tremendous strides over the last two years with the military's funding and he could not afford to lose the big dollars that their contract brought.

In the last year he had isolated the genes involved in repairing damaged tissue in different species of birds and felt he had a workable theory on how these genes could be manipulated to re-grow damaged or even dead tissue. Once he was able to make this gene therapy work on birds he felt he could easily manipulate it with small mammals, primates and then humans.

"Well General, as I have indicated to the Major each week since identifying the "Cosby Genes", as I have dubbed them, I have been looking for ways to increase the rate at which the genes repair and replace damaged or loss tissue."

"And after four weeks you have nothing to show for it?"

"Not entirely," the doctor replied excitedly, "I believe I've had a breakthrough just this week. This way please."

The doctor led the group to a row of cages near the back of the lab. Each of the ten cages held a single pigeon.

"As you know General I was first able to identify the Cosby Genes in several different species of birds. Each of these pigeons has had the left wing surgically removed and then been treated with one of the new gene therapy models I have been working on."

The General stepped forward for a closer look. Starting at the cage labeled CGT-1 he observed single winged pigeons in each cage until he reached cage CGT-7. Peering closer into the cage he saw that the albino pigeon in cage CGT-7 two wings.

"Every pigeon had a wing removed?" the General asked.

"Yes, each and every one of them."

The General moved to the next cage, CGT-7A. One wing. Cages CGT-7B and CGT-7C each also held a pigeon with one wing.

The General moved back to CGT-7 staring intently at the stark white pigeon, "So you would have me believe that this birds' entire wing grew back with your gene therapy?"

"Yes General," the doctor replied proudly.

Holding out his hand the General snapped his fingers, "You have photos of this bird after the wing was removed?"

"Of course," Dr. Cosby quickly retrieved the file folder marked CGT-7 from his desk. Returning to the cages he handed the file the General.

Averting his eyes briefly from the albino pigeon the General flipped through the file.

"And this is the only albino you've had in the lab?"

"Yes General."

"And where do you get your birds from doctor?"

"We trap our own birds locally sir."

"You what?"

"The downtown area is a tremendous breeding ground for pigeons. We feel that by trapping birds here we're saving money on research materials as well as ridding the area of a nuisance."

The General handed the file back to the doctor and paced back and forth in front of the cages, "So you have nine amputee pigeons and one that you say re-grew his wing. Why only one?"

"That's the very question I have been working on General." The doctor moved in between the group and the cages. "Each specimen is labeled CGT, Cosby Gene Therapy, and the formula number. As you can see specimens CGT-1 through 6 had no response to the different models of gene therapy I tried. But with specimen CGT-7 the missing wing was whole again in 72 hours."

"And the three after number 7?"

The doctor took a deep breath, "7A, B and C all received the same therapy model as number 7."

"But no wings?"

The doctor shook his head, "No."

"Why not?"

"Truthfully I don't know yet. It may have something to do with number 7's albinism."

"Why haven't you tried it on another albino?"

"That is the plan as soon as we catch another one. As you know general, true albinos in the wild are quite rare. But we have seen one in the area in recent weeks so it's only a matter of time before we have another test subject."

The General bent over and stared at the albino bird marked CGT-7 before again. The bird in the cage stood perfectly still and peered back at the general unfazed at the close inspection. The general stood and turned towards the door, "You have two weeks to show me similar results on at least two more albinos or you're shut down. Goodbye doctor."

The heavy lab door slammed shut behind the general and his entourage leaving Dr. Cosby alone.

The doctor mumbled, "Two weeks?"

Coming up behind him one of the doctors' lab technicians startled him, "Did you tell the General about the amazing results you've had doctor?"

"Results? Oh yes, the wing re-growth yes."

"The wing?" the tech said shocked, "I mean the bird dying and coming back to life."

"For the last time Ian, the bird did not come back to life…it was in a coma, brought on by the shock of the surgery or the admission of the gene therapy, or a combination of both. If I told the General I had created a zombie pigeon he would shut me down on the spot."

"But Doctor…it wasn't breathing."

"Enough!" the doctor shouted, "We need two more albino pigeons in the next few days or the General shuts us down. Get out and check the traps, and set any additional traps we have available."

"Yes Doctor," the tech replied as he left the lab.

Standing alone in his lab the doctor bent over and looked at pigeon CGT-7, "Zombie pigeon indeed."

Chapter 3

After returning Calliope to her very relieved caretakers Tanners' mom dropped Zoey off at home. After a few hours in the hot Arizona sun Zoey was more then ready for a nice cool shower. The mixed aroma of sweat and sunscreen needed to go.

Coming through the front door she was met by an exuberant Alton, her three year old beagle, jumping into her arms.

"Zoey's home! Zoey's home! Yes, yes, yes, Zoey's home," Alton repeated over and over while licking her face.

"Hello Alton, I missed you too," she said pulling herself away from the wet kisses. Setting him on the ground he excitedly followed her by leaps and bounds to the kitchen.

"Did you find the feather brain?"

"Yes, we found the bird." Zoey added sternly, "You know it's not nice to make fun of other animals. You don't like when cats call you butt-sniffer do you?"

Alton stopped and sat down, "Hey, identification by scent is one of the more advanced forms of identification in the animal kingdom," he said proudly, "Cats wish they could smell as well as dogs."

"I think Mittens next door would disagree with you on that one," Zoey giggled as she poked around the pantry.

Alton started pacing in circles, "Mittens the cat likes to nap in her litter box and besides that…"

Opening the fridge Zoey cut Alton off, "Ok, that's enough. Let's not start the whole dogs are better then cats debate again. I love you and wouldn't trade you for any cat in the world. Do you want a Soy dog?"

Alton tilted his head at her and just stared at her.

Zoey laughed, "You look just like Tanner when you do that."

"What?" he exclaimed.

"I'm only teasing you. Here, this one's a beef hotdog," she said tossing him a cold hot dog.

Alton caught the wiener in mid air and made off to his favorite dining spot under the kitchen table.

Zoey was too hot and tired to even bother heating up her soy dog, eating it straight from the fridge she washed it down with a cold bottle of water. When she was done she started up the stairs toward her room. Pulling the tie out of her ponytail she let her long blonde hair fall around her shoulders. She stopped halfway up the stairs as she usually did to look at the pictures hanging up of her mom.

Zoey really missed her mom. It was still hard to believe that it had been four years since her mom passed away. Zoey was ten at the time and could still remember like it was yesterday the day her mom came home from the doctors and told her she had cancer. Four months later she was gone.

Zoey was very close to her mom and took her passing very hard. In the weeks after her death she became very withdrawn and quiet. She would walk aimlessly around the house or spend hours just sitting at her mom's old desk in the den.

Worried about Zoey spending so much time alone, especially after he went back to work, her dad thought that a companion would be good for Zoey so one day he surprised her with a beagle puppy. Zoey named him Alton, after the host of her mom's favorite cooking show, *Good Eats*. Zoey and her mom would always watch the show together and then try out new dishes from the show.

Alton and Zoey immediately became inseparable and soon after she started opening up again. Despite her dads protests that he should sleep in his kennel the first few days she insisted that Alton sleep in her bed from the very the first night. In a week he was house broken and within a month Alton had mastered all the basic obedience commands; sit, stay, speak, and roll over.

Then one August night something happened that would change her life forever.

The monsoon was in full swing complete with spectacular thunder and lightning storms. Zoey would often times lay with her mom on the hammock on their back porch and watch the amazing displays of blue lightning that the monsoons are known for.

Alton dozed quietly on her lap as Zoey watched the storm from the hammock, stroked the fur on his back and thought about her mom.

Suddenly a bolt of lightning struck the metal frame of the hammock. Zoey felt the shock of the electricity enter her hand, which was resting above her head on the frame and run throughout her entire body like a strong tingly feeling. The shock also caused Alton to jump into the air and into her arms.

"Whoa! You ok boy?" she asked Alton.

"I'm ok, how about you?"

"What did you say?"

Alton tilted his head at her curiously, "I said I'm ok. How are you? Are you ok?"

Zoey stared in disbelief, "I must be dreaming."

"What's dreaming?" Alton asked, "If that was dreaming I sure didn't like it. Please don't dream again."

Zoey held Alton up close to her face, "Alton, you're a dog. You can't talk."

Never one to pass up an opportunity he licked her face, "Of course I can talk, you just can't understand dog."

"But I *can* understand you."

Alton tilted his head again, "Yeah, that is weird."

A crack of thunder drew her attention away from Alton to the night sky, "The lightning hitting the hammock must have done something to me."

"Wait, I'm confused. Was that dreaming or lightning?"

Zoey turned her attention back to Alton. She pulled him close again and stared into his eyes. Again he licked her face.

"I don't care what you call it, I don't like it. Can I go back inside now please?"

Zoey was still in disbelief, "Inside?"

Alton started kicking his legs, "Yeah, lets' go inside and get me one of those doggie ice cream things. I love those!"

She set Alton down on the porch watching him race off through the doggie door into the kitchen. She swung in the hammock in silent disbelief until the sound of Alton's barking snapped her out of it. She turned to see his head sticking out of the doggie door barking at her.

Realizing he was barking at her, not talking she started laughing hysterically, "I knew I was dreaming. Talking to a dog. I must be going crazy."

Zoey stood up and rubbed her face with her hands, "I'm coming boy."

Alton's' head disappeared back into the kitchen and he let out another bark. Zoey took one last look out at the night sky before opening the kitchen door and heading inside.

With Alton yipping at her feet she got a doggie ice cream out of the freezer and placed it in his food dish, "There you go buddy."

"Oh thank you thank you thank you," he replied spinning in circles before diving in to his dish.

In the coming days Zoey would come to learn that she was in fact not dreaming and not only could she understand Alton but a trip to the pet store would confirm that she could understand other animals as well. Mittens, the neighbors' cat would prove to be quite obnoxious in fact. Now she knew why Alton would constantly chase Mittens at every opportunity.

As hard as it was for Zoey to believe that she could understand animals it was twice as hard convincing her best friend Tanner. At first he of course assumed she was joking with him. It finally sank in when she told Tanner to take Alton outside and give him a message to relay to her.

Humoring her Tanner took Alton out in the back yard and sat him on a patio chair, "Ok boy. Pay attention. Tell Zoey that I look nothing like you when I tilt my head at her when I think she is wrong or being weird. You got it boy?"

"Arrf, arrf."

Tanner laughed, "Right, bark, bark. Come on."

Alton jumped off the chair and raced into the house. Tanner took a seat in the patio chair and waited.

A few minutes later Alton came back out through the doggie door and jumped into Tanners' lap. Moments later the kitchen door opened and Zoey joined them.

"Well?" Tanner asked sarcastically.

"Alton agrees that the two of you look nothing alike when you look at me with your head tilted and he is just as bothered by the comparison as you are."

Tanner was in such shock that it took Alton licking his face repeatedly to snap him out of it. But after that Tanner was a believer.

Zoeys' thought was interrupted by her dad coming down the stairs. He gave her a kiss on the forehead and joined her in looking at the pictures of her mom.

Her dad pushed her blonde hair out of her face and back over her right ear, "You look more and more like your mother every day Zo, which means you are going to be one beautiful lady when you grow up."

"Thanks dad."

"Another successful mission for Zoey Zimmerman and Tanner Thompson, Pet Specialists?"

She giggled, "Yes, we found her at South Mountain Park."

"You two are really something else. I don't know how you two do it. You guys have some secret to finding lost pets."

"Just lucky I guess," she replied, "I'm gonna go take a tub Pop."

"Where are you gonna take it?" he laughed continuing down the steps.

She gave him a half hearted laugh, "That joke never gets old dad."

Zoey never told her father about her ability to talk to animals. She thought about it, but since her dad had sent her to a counselor after her mom's death she was afraid that if she told him or the therapist that she could talk to animals that they would think she had lost her mind.

To this day Tanner was the only person she confided her secret to.

After her bath she lay down in bed to take a well deserved nap. Alton joined her in his usual spot at the foot of her bed.

Chapter 4

Rubbing his eyes with the back of his hand Dr. Cosby dropped his identification card twice while trying to swipe it through the card reader to his lab, troubled since the generals' visit the day before the doctor had hardly slept a wink last night.

Setting up a pot of coffee the doctor mumbled to himself, "Two weeks? How can he put work of this magnitude on such a time table? The fool. He should be telling me to take my time, not rush me for results."

The doctor continued his verbal assault on the general while he waited on his coffee. When the pot of coffee was finally full he poured himself a large cup and headed over to his desk.

Glancing over at the bird cages as he passed he was stunned to see more than half the cages were empty. Dropping his coffee on the floor he raced over to the cage marked CGT-7.

Empty!

He rubbed his sleep deprived eyes, hoping beyond hope that he was only dreaming. The only birds still in their cages were birds 7A, 7B and 7C. His lone success, CGT-7 was gone.

"How could this have happened?"

The doctor opened the cage where CGT-7 had been. The cage was spotless.

"Ian!"

The lab tech rushed over, "What's wrong sir?"

"What's wrong?" the doctor replied angrily, "Are you blind fool? The specimens are all gone!"

The tech peered around the doctor, "Gone?"

Furious the doctor grabbed the tech by his lab coat, "Yes gone! And I want to know why!"

"Yessir, r-right away," the tech stuttered pulling away from the enraged doctor.

The doctor stared in disbelief at the empty cage as the tech flipped pages on a clipboard. *All my work, gone.*

"Doctor the log shows that the night crew, um, released the specimens."

"Released?" the doctor shouted, "On whose authority?"

The tech held the clipboard out for the doctor, "Yours' sir."

"Mine?" the doctor replied grabbing the clipboard.

"Yes sir."

The doctor ran his finger down the list of specimens; each had a checkmark in the "remove" column, including CGT-7. At the bottom of the page were the doctors' own initials authorizing the removal of all the marked birds.

"What have I done?' the doctor muttered, "I was here so late last night, I must have been more tired than I thought."

"It may not be too late doctor," the tech interrupted, "The birds may still be in the facility."

"Still here? Where?"

"The specimen room, any usable specimens are taken to the specimen room and held for other research if needed."

"Of course," the doctor replied excitedly, "Lets' go."

***

The tech swiped his card into the reader at the specimen room and hurriedly pushed the door open with the doctor right on his heels.

As the tech looked for the specimen room log the doctor began scouring the rooms cages one by one, looking for his precious CGT-7. Not seeing his bird among the many pigeon filled cages the doctor desperately turned towards the tech, "I don't see it anywhere."

As he looked up form the log the doctor could tell by the techs face that it was not good news, "I'm sorry sir."

"No, no, no…why?"

"It appears that there was no more room for more specimens so the ones that came from your lab were released sir. I'm sorry."

The doctor was crushed.

"There seems to be another problem sir."

What else can go wrong?

"The notes on the log say that two of the birds, CGT-3 and CGT-4, were put in the transport cage with CGT -7. The notes say that the two gray pigeons had been pecked to death by CGT-7."

"Strange," the doctor replied.

"Even stranger; notes later in the log state that CGT-7 and the two other birds were all released at the same time."

"What are you talking about man?" the doctor said grabbing the clipboard and skimming the notes for him self.

The tech pointed out a section of the log:

Time: 10:34 pm.
Notes: Specimen CGT-7 killed specimens CGT-3 and CGT-4 while in transit from lab to specimen room.
Employee Initials: EM

He then flipped to the next page:

Time: 11:41 pm.
Notes: Specimens CGT-3, CGT-4 & CGT-7 released.
Employee Initials: AC

"So, EM made a mistake, the specimens could not have been killed if they were later released as the log shows."

"But sir, what if they were killed and came back to life just like CGT-7?"

"Again with your zombie pigeon theory? Nonsense! I swear I do not know where we get some of the techs around here. They can't tell the difference between a dead pigeon and a live one."

"But Doctor…"

"Enough!" The doctor placed his hands on the counter and hung his head. Not only did he have two weeks in which to duplicate his lone success, but now his lone success was gone. The general would shut him down now for sure, "It's hopeless."

"Maybe not sir."

"What do you mean?" the doctor asked.

"Well sir, it may seem silly, but there may be something we can do."

Excitedly the doctor again grabbed the tech by his lab coat, "Well spit it out man!"

"Well sir, my sisters new cockatoo had recently flown out of the house and gotten lost and, well they had hired someone to track it down and find it for them. My sister swears by them."

The doctors' mind raced. It definitely was a long shot that the bird could be found, but without CGT-7 it was almost certain that the general would shut the doctor down immediately. It was a small glimmer of hope, but at least it was better then nothing.

"Yes, do it. Contact this animal tracker. The sooner they start the better."

"Yes sir. I'll get the number from my sister and try to have them her this afternoon."

The doctor gave the tech a pat on the shoulder before hurrying back to his lab, "Good man…yes, I'll be in my lab."

Chapter 5

Tanner was shooting hoops in the driveway when his mom called him, "Tanner! Zoey just called…she says you two have another job. We're picking her up in 20 minutes."

Tanner sighed. His mom was always ready and willing to drive him and Zoey around for their various lost pet "jobs." He wished that just for once she would say she couldn't drive them to a job, but he knew that wasn't likely to happen since she was too much of a pet lover herself.

"Can't you tell her that it's too hot out for us to be working outside today?"

"I already told her you were outside playing basketball."

He figured as much, but it was worth a try. Tanner just hoped that this job would not result in the two of them hiking around the desert again.

Why can't someone ever lose their dog at the mall or the water park? He wondered to himself as he headed in to get ready to go.

***

Tanners' mom honked the car horn as they pulled up in front of Zoey's house. Alton as usual was the first out as he popped out the doggie door. The front door opened and Zoey followed, "Slow down Alton."

Alton couldn't help it, he was so excited. He hadn't gone for a car ride in weeks and couldn't wait to stick his head out the window. "Hurry Zoey, hurry," he said to her, running in circles on the sidewalk waiting for Zoey to catch up.

"Don't make me change my mind about taking you with us," Zoey warned.

Heeding the warning Alton stopped in his tracks and sat down.

Zoey gave him a pat on the head, "That's better," and opened the back door of the car.

Alton barked and jumped in the car, quickly landing in Tanners lap, repeatedly licking his face.

Tanner tugged on Alton's' collar in a vain attempt to pull him away, "Ok boy, good to see you too. Stop with the slobbering."

Climbing in the car Zoey took Alton's face in her hands and looked him straight in the eye, "Are you coming with or are you staying home?"

"Coming with."

"Then lay down please." Alton complied and settled in between Tanner and Zoey.

"Here's the address Mrs. Thompson," Zoey said handing her a slip of paper.

"Thank you dear," she replied looking at the address, "Oh, that's downtown, near Chase Field."

Tanner's eyes lit up, "Chase Field?"

Zoey rolled her eyes, "Here we go."

"We should definitely check Chase Field first Zo."

"Tank, what makes you think what we are looking for is gonna be there?"

"Because the Diamondbacks are playing later today."

Chase Field was the home of the Arizona Diamondbacks, Tanners favorite baseball team. He would use any excuse to make a trip to

Chase Field, especially if the Diamondbacks were playing, even if it was only to hang out near the players' parking lot entrance hoping to catch a glance of one of his favorite players.

"Besides, we have the reward money from Calliope, and we deserve some fun for our selves."

Tanner had a good argument. They did get $50 for finding Calliope, and the idea of some nachos in the bleachers at a baseball game was tempting, "Ok, I'll make you a deal. If we either find this bird or we have absolutely no leads by the time the game starts we'll go. Deal?"

Tanner pumped his fist, "Yes! What are we looking for anyways?"

Zoey handed Tanner a sheet of notebook paper.

"FutureCore Industries? Albino research pigeon?"

Knowing how many pigeons there were in the Phoenix area Tanner sank in his seat as he felt the prospect of seeing his beloved Diamondbacks fly away.

Chapter 6

Tanners' mom the pair gave a wave as she drove away and mouthed the words, "Call me."

Tanner held the door to FutureCore Industries open for Zoey, "Always the gentleman, thank you."

"You're welcome", Tanner followed her in.

The lobby to FutureCore was enormous, but empty and sterile; with only a small desk with a lone guard sitting at the far end from the entrance.

The guard, a chubby older man with shaggy gray hair and a bushy mustache to match looked up from his paper and shouted in a grainy voice, "You kids are in the wrong place. You need to leave."

Zoey and Tanner exchanged nervous glances before they stepped forward and Zoey spoke, "We are here to see Ian in Dr. Cosby's office."

The guard gave them a grumpy look before picking up the phone, "Let me call and check. Name?"

"Our names?" Zoey asked.

Clearly agitated he guard growled sarcastically, "No, your dogs name."

Excited to be noticed Alton began bouncing up and down, "Alton! My name is Alton."

Of course all the guard heard was barking.

This of course made Tanner laugh.

That of course made the guard grumpier, "Somethin' funny boy?"

Tanner bit his lip and composed himself.

"I'm sorry, they don't get out much. My name is Zoey Zimmerman."

Putting the receiver to his ear the guard spun his chair turning his back on the teens as he mumbled into the phone.

After a few moments the guard spun back around and faced them. He slammed the phone back down on its base. Pointing to his left the guard growled, "Take the elevator down to B1. Turn right when you get off the elevator. And that dog had better not make any messes while he is here."

Alton again barked at the guard, but what Zoey heard was, "Make a mess? I'll have you know I've been housebroken for years!"

Zoey tugged on his leash, "Alton, shush."

Tanner pressed the down button for the elevator and as they waited the guard gave one final warning, "Remember, we do have animal research here...I'm sure we could always find a use for an over hyper canine."

Zoey, Tanner and Alton all swallowed hard as they stepped into the elevator. As the door closed Tanner asked, "What have you gotten us into now Zo?"

Zoey shook her head as the elevator door closed, "I don't know."

Chapter 7

The elevator doors opened and Zoey and Tank were greeted by a man in a white lab coat, "Hello, my name is Ian."

Zoey extended her hand, "Hi, I'm Zoey, this is Tanner."

Ian, obviously perplexed slowly extended his hand in return, "I think there's been some kind of mistake, I was expecting…"

"Grown ups," Tank interrupted, "We get that a lot. It's ok."

"Yes, well, the missing bird is very important to our research here, so I'm very sorry that you made the trip for nothing, but I think that I'll call someone," he paused, "A little older."

Zoey and Tanner were used to skeptical adults and as always was prepared, handing Ian a sheet of paper, "Before we go if you would take a look at this list of references you'll see that we find most animals in less than two days."

"Two days?" Ian said taking the reference list from her. He pondered whether or not the doctor would approve of the fate of his research being placed in the hands of these children. Probably not, but looking at their reference sheet he could not argue with their results, especially the last name on the list; his sisters.

"Ok," Ian sighed, "Come with me."

Ian swiped his ID card thru a slot by the door. *I'll give them 24 hours* he thought to himself.

***

Ian led Zoey and Tanner through the lab cooing, passing by the numerous cages full of cooing pigeons, "The missing specimen is an albino pigeon. It is very important to our research here."

Zoey knew that animal research went on in the world and that it was a necessary evil, but she would never be part of cruel animal research, and that included returning missing specimens.

"What kind of research do you do here?" Zoey asked.

"This particular bird is vital to our cancer research," Ian replied.

Zoey was trying to pay attention to Ian, but it was very difficult with all the noise, she did however catch the word "cancer". While all Tanner and Ian heard was cooing sounds coming from the caged birds Zoey was having a hard time ignoring all the conversations that were really taking place.

"Is it time to eat yet? When is it time to eat again?"

"You're always hungry."

"I'm hungry too, is it time to eat?"

"I wonder who those kids are."

"Whose kids?"

"Those kids."

"You think he's going to tell them about the zombie pigeon?"

"What's a zombie?"

"Is a zombie food?"

"The zombie has food?"

"You're always hungry."

Zoey usually did not pay much attention to animal mumblings, especially wild animals like birds. Their conversations did not always make sense and this time was no exception. What could they have been talking about a zombie pigeon? They must have the wrong word.

The chatter among the birds got Alton riled up and talking as well, "Is it time to eat? I'm hungry too. DO you like being called kids? What is a zombie? Is a zombie a kind of sandwich? I'm hungry. Is it time to eat?"

"Yo Zo, you still with us?" Tanner asked.

Zoey tried tuning out Alton and the birds, "Yes. Alton, please."

She took a deep breath, "You know how it is."

Tanner knew all too well that I in with all the bird cages here and with Alton tagging along that this was just like a rock concert that only Zoey could hear.

"Here is a picture of the bird and this paper has the serial numbers of the bands on each of the birds' legs," Ian said as he handed Tanner a Polaroid and a sheet of paper. Tanner looked at the photo of the all white pigeon with bright red eyes. The bird had a metal band on each of its pink legs, one red and one blue.

"What kind of research do you do here sir?" Tanner asked.

Ian was startled by the question, "We, um, well its classified actually."

"I could tell you but I'd have to kill you kind of stuff huh?" Tanner joked.

"What? No, of course not, no," the nervous tech replied.

Zoey gave Tanner an elbow to the side, "He's just kidding."

Zoey gave Tanner a stern look and he gestured back, *what?*

"How long has the bird been missing?"

"Well he was accidentally released sometime during the night between midnight and five in the morning."

The chatter from the caged birds grew louder.

"He's talking about the zombie pigeon."

"Who's talking?"

"What's a zombie?"

"Is it time to eat yet?"

"Its time to eat?"

"I'm hungry."

"You're always hungry."

The chatter from the caged birds was starting to give Zoey a headache, the lab in general gave her the creeps and she really wanted to go.

"We'll get right on it if you can just give us a phone number to contact you by."

"It's on the paper with the band serial numbers," Ian replied.

"We'll be in touch," Tanner said, trying his best trying to sound professional.

Ian led the trio out of the lab and back to the elevator. He slid his card through the reader opening the door and then pressed the button for the lobby.

Chapter 8

The elevator door had barely shut when Alton started pestering Zoey, "What is a zombie pigeon Zoey, what is it? Is it a sandwich? I'd try a zombie pigeon sandwich, except for the beak. Do they take the beak off on a zombie pigeon?"

Zoey's head was already pounding from all the racket inside the lab and Alton was just making it worse, "Alton, please stop."

Alton's butt hit the floor and he drooped his head, "Sorry."

As per usual Tanner had no idea what was going on so he asked, "What's up with Alton?"

"I'm not sure," Zoey replied still trying to ease her headache by rubbing her temples, "He keeps asking what a zombie pigeon is. The birds in the lab were talking about it."

"Zombie pigeon? What the heck does that mean?"

Zoey took a deep breath and let it out slowly before answering, "I have no idea. I'm guessing the pigeons in the lab got a word that sounds like zombie mixed up."

"You sure it's not a sandwich?" Alton asked.

Zoey didn't answer him but did give him a stern look which prompted him to quietly lie down.

"I don't know Zo; this is a lab that does animal experiments. What if they brought this pigeon back to life and…"

Zoey held her hand up cutting him off, "Tank please, my head is killing me."

The elevator doors opened at the main lobby. Alton jumped up and ran out the elevator.

"I'm sorry but you've seen *Night of the Living Dead.*"

Zoey shouted, "Tank!" Her shout drew the attention of the grumpy security guard from behind his newspaper.

The duo quickly made for the door before he could roust them again. Pushing open the glass double doors Tanner stood up against one of the doors to let Zoey out. He tried his best to mangle his face, his jaw gaping open. He pulled his elbows in close to his body and held his hands up in front of his chest with all his fingers bent to give the appearance of severe arthritis.

Zoey tried to ignore him as she passed by him, but could not help but giggle and shake her head at his appearance.

Once she was through the door Tanner followed behind her walking very slowly and with a slight limp. He started making moaning noises, "Ugghhh. Ugh Alll-ton. All-ton."

Hearing his name Alton stopped and looked up at Tanner who was stalking towards him.

Alton let out a yelp and quickly hid behind a near y mailbox. He poked his head out from behind the box and gave a low growl.

Surprised at his reaction Zoey scolded him, "Alton, you stop that this instant."

She gave Tanner a smack on the arm as well, "And you too. Seriously, I wonder why I bring you two along sometimes."

Tanner returned to normal and let out a big laugh pointing at the beagle still hiding behind the mailbox, "You were really scared Alton."

"Was not," Alton replied slowly walking back to join them. Of course Tanner was not able to hear his denial, but he assumed there was one.

"What did he say," Tanner asked still giggling.

"Nothing," she replied clipping his leash to his collar.

"Yes I did," Alton said, "I said I wasn't scared."

"He said something."

"Ok, so Chase field is just two blocks over right," Zoey said, hoping a change in subject would get her out of the middle of the dog versus boy battle of wits.

Tanner tugged at the brim of his Arizona Diamondbacks baseball cap atop his head and headed off towards the ballpark, "It sure is. I can smell the hotdogs from here."

Hearing his favorite word in the whole world, hotdogs, Alton ran after tanner, "I smell hotdogs too. Do you think they have zombie dogs?"

Zoey cupped her face with both hands and sighed before following after them.

***

Zoey, Tanner and Alton waited patiently across the street from Chase Field waiting for the stop light to change. Tanner bounced with excitement at the site of the ball park. Looking at her watch Zoey held out hope that they either found the missing pigeon very quickly or they could produce absolutely no leads. Game time was 6:20 p.m. and her watch read 12:18 p.m. She knew that in a few hours Tanner would start dropping hints about the game and she knew as the first pitch grew nearer it would be harder to keep Tanner focused on the job at hand.
"So besides the fact that I wanted to hang out here, what made you decide to start looking here Zo?"

"Well with the roof open it's the biggest grass field around here and with the number of garbage dumpsters out back odds are the bird will either be here or there will be enough other birds here to ask if they have seen him."

"Makes sense," Tanner replied.

"Plus this way you won't be whining about when can we go to the ballpark."

Tanner tilted his head, closed one eye and gave her a grin.

"Your right, he does look like me when he does that," Alton blurted out.

The light turned from DON'T WALK to WALK and Alton took off pulling Zoey behind him on his leash.

Tanner knew from Zoeys' laugh that Alton had said something, "What? What did he say?"

Ignoring his question Zoey sped up to a run and heading towards the ballpark laughing, leaving Tanner behind at the sidewalk looking bewildered.

"What did he say?"

Left out of the joke once again Tanner could only shrug his shoulders and follow the giddy duo across the street.

Chapter 9

Mitch exited the elevator at the roof level of Chase Field and let out a deep sigh. Being slightly afraid of heights he hated coming up here for inspection.

With the extreme temperatures of the Sonoran Desert of the Southwest the baseball stadium was built with a retractable roof that would allow for both open air and indoor stadium events. While the stadium was a modern marvel of architecture the roof required constant inspections to ensure proper operation.

Those inspections were normally handled by one of Mitch's' employees, but with one on vacation and the other at a conference that left today's inspection up to Mitch. Most of the inspection was no problem for him. It was walking out and inspecting the points on the catwalk, high above the field that put a knot in his stomach.

Mitch never rushed or did a less than proper inspection, he also did not dilly dally around on the catwalks. Staring from the south end of the stadium he made his way across the catwalk on the east side of the stadium. He unclipped his safety line from the east catwalk and made his way over to the west catwalk.

He proceeded on his inspection as he headed for the west catwalk. The walk was long enough for the knot in his stomach to loosen up just in time for a new one to form as he clipped on his safety line to the west catwalk.

As he neared the end of the second catwalk he could see several pigeons up ahead on the walkway, which was not unusual.

There was one white pigeon and two gray pigeons sitting on the same hand rail that his safety line was hooked to and oddly enough another gray pigeon lying on its side on the floor of the catwalk. Mitch continued along waiting for the birds to fly away but as he inched closer the birds remained still. Mitch was now just three feet from the pigeons and not only they not moved, but they didn't even seem to notice him.

The pigeon at his feet appeared lifeless as he stepped forward and passed over it. He would need to make a note for someone to come up with a trash bag to remove it. Looking back up at the pigeons on the rail Mitch was stopped dead in his tracks and the hair stood up on the back of his neck. The pigeons had finally noticed him and each had turned their head towards Mitch. The birds were literally staring at him as they never blinked their white eyes.

White eyes? Do pigeons have white eyes? He thought to himself.

Mitch stood motionless in an eerie stare down with the bird trio. If they did not move Mitch would have to undo his safety line and switch it to the opposite railing. Not a thought he relished this high up.

Mitch waved his hand, "Shoo bird. Shoo."

The pigeons remained motionless.

"Come one. Beat it. Shoo."

Nothing.

"At least blink you creepy bird."

Not wanting to dawdle on the catwalk any longer than he had to Mitch finally unlatched his safety line and quickly reattached it on the opposite rail and continued on. The birds completely ignored Mitch as he passed by.

Mitch continued along with his inspection when he heard scratching and wings flapping behind him. He turned to see the gray pigeon on the floor of the catwalk was now standing up and looking his direction.

Well that was just weird. He thought to himself as he unlatched his safety line.

And another pigeon with white eyes.

Turning for one last look at the group of birds a shudder ran down his spine as he saw nothing but an empty catwalk.

Boy do I hate coming up here.

Chapter 10

Zoey and Tanner made their way around to the back of the stadium where they figured the garbage dumpsters would most likely be at. Even if the missing bird itself was not at the dumpsters there was a good chance that there would be at least one or two wild birds that may have seen it in the area.

At the south end of the stadium the players' entrance also led to the back of the stadium. Unfortunately standing in their way was a very large security guard. Zoey knelt down beside Alton and unhooked his leash.

"Ok pal, you know the drill."

Alton sat down and looked up at Zoey with his best "puppy dog eyes."

"Oh come one," Zoey pleaded, "Your not really going to make me say it are you?"

Being in on the joke this time Tanner nudged Zoey with his elbow, "Come on, do it."

Zoey knew some days there was just no arguing with these two.

"All right, all right," she sighed, "We have a 'Code Alpha' in progress."

Tanner laughed as Alton's ears perked up and he made a bead straight for the security guard, "Yippee!"

Slowly she turned her head towards Tanner and frowned, "Why did you have to teach him that?"

Tanner was laughing uncontrollably now.

"You have my dog thinking he is a special ops dog with that 'Code Alpha' stuff you know."

"I know, it's awesome," he replied still trying to control his laughing.

"Why do we need a code word anyway for a dog distraction?"

"Because its fun."

Boys. How do I put up with these two some days she thought grabbing Tanner by his sleeve and pulling him after Alton, "Come on."

Barking for attention Alton ran down the sidewalk directly at the security guard. Alton quickly ran circles around the confused guard before running past him and down the driveway towards the back of the stadium. With a car pulling up to the gate and trying to keep several autograph hunters from rushing the cars the guard was not able to go after Alton.

Running past the gate Zoey started her best fake tears, "Alton, Alton, come back here."

"Hey kid, you can't go back there," the guard shouted.

"But my dog, that's my dog," she cried.

Grabbing the guard by the shirt Tanner shouted, "Our dog, that's our dog!"

Between the crowd of fans shouting at the player in the car, the player honking his horn for the gate to be opened coupled with Zoey and Tanners shouting was overwhelming the guard.

Pushing Tanner back and straightening his shirt the guard pointed down the driveway, "You two get that dog and get out of here or I'm calling the cops."

Tanner gave a quick salute before following Zoey and Alton, "Yessir!"

Once around the corner and out of the guards' sight Zoey stopped and called out for Alton to come back, "Good job Alton, come here boy!"

Alton jumped into her arms and started licking her face, "I love Code Alpha!"

"Ok, ok, good boy," she replied setting him down, "Now where's Tanner?"

"Right here," he replied coming around the corner, "We better hurry. The guard threatened to call the cops if we didn't get Alton and get out of here."

Zoey wiped the slobber off her face with a tissue, "Ok. Alton, can you sniff out the garbage dumpster's boy?"

Alton sat again and looked up at her with those eyes.

"There is no code for sniffing garbage," she shouted and stamped her foot, "Just go."

Startled by her stomping her foot Alton ran off, "Well there should be a code!"

"We could always use 'Code Gamma' for garbage hunt," Tanner cracked running off behind Alton.

Zoey stomped her foot again, "There's no code for garbage!"

Chapter 11

Dr. Cosby slid his key card threw the slot but the indicator light stayed red. Impatiently he swiped the card a second and then a third time, but still the light stayed red. Angrily he started hitting the card reader with the clip board he was holding.

"That will be enough doctor."

Dr. Cosby froze at the sound of General Lucas' voice. He took a deep breath and composed himself before turning to face the general, "Still in town General?"

"Actually I was on my way back to Washington when I was called back here by Major Lee."

Dr. Cosby suddenly realized something was very wrong. Standing behind General Gibson and Major Lee were several people he did not recognize as FutreCore staff dressed in blue lab coats and half a dozen military policemen. His lab assistant Ian was also present.

"I-is there a problem General?" the doctor stuttered, "I thought you gave me two weeks?"

"That was before we received some disturbing news from here."

Ian stepped forward, "I'm sorry doctor, but I had to inform the Major of the possible risk of an infection escaping the lab."

Stepping forward Dr. Cosby now realized that logo on the blue lab coats said CDC. Center for Disease Control.

"Infection? What infection?"

Ian held up a blue computer disc.

Dr. Cosby immediately recognized it as his private notes disc that he kept separate from the official FutureCore database. Now he knew why the General was here with the military police. He was about to go to jail.

"Ian how could you?"

"I'm sorry doctor. I knew you were keeping something from me and the more I thought about sending those two kids after your lost pigeon I had to know what it was. When I read your notes it was even worse then I feared. I had to inform the Major."

The General placed a hand on Ian's shoulder, "You did the right thing son."

"No, you don't understand. My research…"
"Is over Doctor," the General cut him off, "This whole lab is shut down until the CDC examines every employee, every computer file and every experiment and gives an all clear."

The doctor dropped his clipboard and cupped his face in his hands as tears began to flow.

The General motioned to the MPs, "Take the doctor into custody please."

Ian felt a combination of guilt and remorse as the doctor was led away in handcuffs. He turned to the General and handed him the blue disc.

The General handed the disc off to one of the CDC doctors, "Get on this right away. If what Ian told us is correct we have a potential undead infection on the loose. We will need to start the Romero Protocols right away."

Knowing their respective assignments the CDC staff and MPs all quickly dispersed at the generals' orders.

Ian was very confused, "The Government has protocols in place for a real zombie epidemic?"

"That information is classified," the Major said, "But lets' just say that sometimes it's easier to cover something up by making a popular movie about it to make it more unbelievable."

Ian was in shock, "Are you saying that zombies really exist?"

"There's no time for this right now Ian," the General interrupted handing Ian a blue lab coat, "All in good time. Right now we need to talk about your new job with the CDC and finding these kids before they find the doctors zombie pigeon."

Ian took the lab coat and put it on, "Thank you General. About the kids, after I read the doctors private notes I tried to call them to cancel their services. But it seems that the doctor erased the phone logs that contained the phone number for them."

"Major, get a full description of the kids from Ian and send out an all points bulletin to local law enforcement," the General ordered, "I want those kids found as soon as possible."

"Yes sir," the Major replied handing the General an iPad.

"Uh, General, the doctors' notes did contain a file on a possible antivirus to the formula that was used on the zombie pigeon," Ian said, "I did not read it in detail, but it is there."

"Good work, get to work on it right away," the General typed into his iPad. Suddenly the red light on the doctor office door turned from red to green.

"The doctors' office is now yours Ian," the General said handing him back the blue disc, "If there is an antigen for the doctors new virus CDC is going to need to produce it and a means of administering it on both a small and large scale. Keep the Major posted on your progress."

"Yes sir," Ian replied as he hurried into his new office to start working on the antivirus.

Chapter 12

"Oh man that reeks," Tanner said holding his nose.

"Well 40,000 people at a game make a lot of trash, but it also makes for a lot of pigeon food," Zoey joked.

"Ugh gross, just talk to the bird brains so we can get out of here. I'll be up-wind. Come on Alton, lets' find some shade."

Tanner and Alton waited patiently as Zoey made her way around the dumpsters, showing the picture of the missing bird and talking to small groups of pigeons, sparrows and even a few crows. Fifteen minutes later she was still going around to different birds. *Usually this doesn't take very long. I wonder what's up?* Tanner wondered.

Another ten minutes went by before Zoey finally came over. Tanner could tell by the look on her face that she was worried about something.

"What's up Zo? Any of them see our bird?"

"Yes, our bird was here not very long ago," she replied, "But something really weird is going on."

"What?"

Zoey pointed at the birds around the dumpsters, "They're all saying that the bird was here and that it pecked a few birds to death, but then a little while later the dead birds got back up. They flew inside the stadium maybe a half hour ago. All three of them had white eyes."

"Zombie pigeons?"

"That's ridiculous," Zoey said half heartedly.

"That's what the caged birds at the lab were talking about?" Tanner shouted.

"Do you know how crazy that sounds?"

"They sent us after a zombie pigeon Zo!"

"We better call that guy Ian from the lab," Zoey said opening up her cell phone she dialed Ian's number.

Their conversation was interrupted by the sound of one of the stadium garage doors opening up.

"Code Alpha, inside we go," Alton shouted running off inside the stadium.

"Alton no," Zoey shouted to no avail. He was already inside.

"Tank after him!" Zoey shouted closing his flip phone.

"But, the zombie pigeon. Ian!"

"We have to get Alton first!" she shouted running inside the stadium, "Alton stop!"

"This is so not good," Tanner replied as he followed into the stadium.

Chapter 13

Ian was working feverishly when the office door opened and the Major entered, "Status update Ian?"

"Yes Major. It seems the doctor was much further along then I thought. Not only is there an anti-virus formula but there are notes on a possible large scale application, well at least a large scale bird application. There would need to be more work done if we had to roll out the anti-virus to humans."

"Is someone working on the anti-virus now?"

Ian pointed out to the lab, "Yes, I have three techs working on the anti-virus now. From the notes it is around a two hour process to produce. They have been on it for about an hour."

"And the large scale application?"

"Um well, yes. Bird seed."

"Bird seed?"

"Yes, the anti-virus would be applied to a batch of bird seed, which when ingested would immunize an un-infected bird and theoretically "cure" an infected one."

"Theoretically?" the Major questioned.

"Well yes sir, the doctors notes don't list any trials, so it is all the theoretical. That's the best I can give right now."

"Very well, I'll inform the General of your progress. I'll be back in an hour," the Major said as he left the office.

As the office door closed Ian's cell phone rang, but stopped before he could answer it. He looked at the caller ID and not recognizing the number went back to work.

Unknown Caller
623-555-1138

Chapter 14

Zoey and Tanner tried to catch up to Alton to no avail. He was just to fast and had a head start. They had already lost site of him and if not for his barking and shouting 'Code Alpha' they wouldn't even know which way to turn to follow him. They were now deep underneath the stadium, which was a maze of hallways.

"Zoey, we really shouldn't be in here," Tanner whispered.

"I know," she fired back, "We need to find Alton, call that Ian guy and get out of here."

The hallway suddenly filled with the echoing sounds of dog toe nails running on the cold tile floor and Alton turned a corner and continued running towards them. Seeing Zoey and Tanner Alton slid to stop and shouted excitedly, "I found them I found them! This way."

Of course all Tanner heard was barking.

Before Zoey could say anything Alton quickly disappeared again back around the corner shouting, "Follow me, follow me!"

"Alton no, come back!"

Zoey ran off after Alton just as an office door opened to Tanners right. Standing in the door was a large man in a Diamondbacks uniform. Tanner easily recognized him as Diamondbacks outfielder Greg Steele.

"Was that a dog barking? Hey what are you kids doing in here?"

Struck by a combination of fear and awe Tanner was frozen in his tracks.

"How did you get in here son?"

"Um, I can explain, I think. But your so not gonna believe me Mr. Steele."

* * *

Zoey followed the sound of Alton's barking down a long hallway. The light at the end of the hallway was far brighter and she quickly realized why. At the end of the hallway she found herself walking into the pitchers bullpen located out in left field. With the roof open the stadium was bright as day. She had to shield her eyes from the bright light in order to see.

Scanning the bullpen she didn't see Alton anywhere, "Alton where are you?"

Alton quickly appeared at the door of the bullpen that led directly out into left field, "Right here Zoey! I found them!"

Alton then ran off again out into the field.

"Alton stop, come back here, please," Zoey pleaded as she followed him reluctantly onto the field, "I think those birds might be dangerous."

Alton either couldn't hear her or he was too excited to listen as he just kept running out towards centerfield shouting, "This way, this way!"

Alton finally stopped in left centerfield and Zoey was finally able to catch up to him. Alton squirmed as she picked him up, "Alton that was very bad."

"But I found them," he replied licking her face.

Zoey put her hand over is snout to keep his slobbering at bay, "Found who?"

"The zombie pigeons. Look."

Zoey looked down to see not only the albino pigeon they were looking for but at least a dozen other pigeons as well. She guessed maybe ten feet separated her from the birds. The pigeons didn't move and made no sounds, they just stared at her with their bizarre milky white eyes.

A shiver went down her spine and Zoey started to slowly step backwards when she heard the fluttering of wings behind her. Turning around she realized that she was now surrounded by dozens and dozens of white eyed pigeons. There was not a single direction she could walk without having to pass by the eerie birds. She was trapped.

The silence was suddenly broken by the sound of helicopter blades roaring and metal gears turning. Zoey looked up to see a green army helicopter hovering above the stadium. Below the copter the retractable stadium roof was closing.

Alton barked, "Get back bird!"

Zoey turned her attention back to the ground and realized that the birds were slowly walking towards her, closing the gap between them.

Zoey thought back to what the bids at the garbage dumpster had told her about the zombie pigeon pecking other birds to death and wondered if she was next.

Suddenly she heard Tanners familiar voice shouting her name, "Zoey!"

Zoey turned to her right to see Tanner riding shotgun in a golf cart driven by a large man in a Diamondbacks jersey, heading right towards her.
"Zoey get ready to jump in!" Tanner shouted sticking his thumb out towards the back of the cart.

As they rumbled closer Zoey could see what Tanner was pointing at. The golf cart was only a two-seater, but had a pick up truck like bed on the back of it.

Alton's' continued barking did nothing to dissuade the approach of the zombie pigeons. Zoey held her dog tight as she awaited the arrival of the rescue cart.

"Go go go," Tanner shouted.

Not even the approaching golf cart phased the zombie pigeons. They paid it no attention as they lumbered towards her.

"Look out," the large man shouted.

Several pigeons bounced off the front of the cart as the driver slammed on the breaks coming to stop right next to Zoey.

Kicking a pigeon out of the way herself Zoey tossed the Alton into the back of the cart and jumped in herself.

"She's in, go!" Tanner yelled.

"We're outta her," the driver replied as he revved the cart back up and left the pigeons behind.

Zoey tapped Tanner on the shoulder, "Um Tank."

Tanner turned in his seat to see Zoey pointing behind them at the flock of zombie pigeons flying after them.

"Step on it!" Tanner shouted.

The driver turned and saw the "rabid" pigeons chasing after them, "Consider it stepped on!"

The golf cart raced for the bullpen opening, zombie pigeons in close pursuit, Zoey and Tanner could only sit silently and watch as the birds closed the gap between them. The albino pigeon was in the lead and was quickly catching up to the golf cart.

Alton's' warning bark went ignoring as the birds continued on. Zoey closed her eyes and held Alton tight.

Zoey heard a loud bang. Opening her eyes she saw the zombie pigeon was engulfed in black netting as it fell to the ground.

Several more loud blasts filled the air. She watched as more birds fell to the ground in the black netting. Looking around Zoey and Tanner were shocked to see dozens of soldiers dressed in black scattered about. Some carried machine guns while many others carried nets and cages of varying sizes as they chased pigeons around the outfield.

Zoey and Tanner exchanged a glance of relief as they sat back in the golf cart.

Chapter 15

Zoey took deep breath before sitting up in the bed of the golf cart, "That was a close one Tank."

"You two okay?" Tanner asked.

"Yeah, we're good now," she replied, "Thanks a lot mister."

"No problem kid," the driver replied, "I didn't even know pigeons could get rabies."

"Rabies?" Zoey asked looking at Tanner.

He winked back, "Yeah Zo, raaa-bies."

Zoey understood right away. Rabies would be a lot easier to explain then zombie pigeons.

As the golf cart approached the bullpen they came to a stop and two soldiers ushered them out of the cart and back under the stadium.

Zoey was still trying to figure out what was happening when she recognized a familiar face in a blue lab coat, "Ian?"

"Yes, I am so glad we found you two," he replied.

"But how did you find us?"

"Tanner put his arm around her shoulder, "Zoey meet Greg Steele. He's the outfield for the Diamondbacks."

Greg shook her hand, "Pleased to meet you."

I explained to him about the "rabies" outbreak and he helped me find the phone number for FutureCore and we got a hold of Ian."

Ian extended his hand to the manager, "Thank you so much Mr. Steele. We'll take it from here and we should be all cleared out of the stadium well before game time."

"My pleasure, I'm just glad no one got hurt," Greg turned to Zoey and Tanner, "How would you kids like to stay for the ball game tonight?"

Tanners' eyes lit up and there was no way Zoey could turn him down, "We'd love to."

"Yes," Tanner shouted and gave Greg a high five.

"Ok Tank, you know where the clubhouse is. You come by when your done here and I'll give you two a tour of the stadium before the game."

With that the outfielder left the duo with Ian.

"Awesome thanks," Tanner replied.

Zoey looked at Tanner, "Tank huh?"

"So maybe I told him he could call me Tank."

"Boys," Zoey laughed.

Chapter 16

Zoey and Tanner watched from the bullpen as the soldiers rounded up all the milky eyed birds and handed them off to the people in the blue lab coats. With the roof closed there was no way for the infected birds to get back outside, it was all just a matter of rounding them up.

Zoey turned to Ian, "Are they really zombie pigeons?"

The look of shock on Ian's' face was apparent, "What makes you say that?"

"Yes young lady, what makes you say that," a deep voice asked from behind them.

All the soldiers suddenly came to attention and saluted as General Lucas approached. One of the soldiers handed the general piece of paper, "Their names and numbers sir."

The General took the piece of paper containing Zoey and Tanners names and cell phone numbers, "Carry on men," the General saluted back and the soldiers went back to work.

Ian motioned to the General, "Kids this is General Lucas, he is in charge here. You should tell him what you know."

Zoey and Tanner exchanged a glance and he nodded his head.

"I can," she paused, "I have a gift. I can talk to animals. I heard some of the birds at the lab talking about zombie pigeons, and then outside the stadium here some birds told me that the white pigeon had attacked other birds that became infected too."

The General turned to Ian, "Ian please go make sure that the anti-virus seeds are placed all around the outside of the stadium as well as in the grass inside the field as well."

Ian understood he was being told politely to leave, "Yes General."

The General waited for Ian to be out of sight, "Is there anything else about these zombie pigeons you heard?"

"No sir, that's about it."

"Very well," the General folded up the piece of paper with their names on it and placed it in his coat pocket. He reached into another pocket and pulled out a business card that he handed to Zoey. The card was plain white and only contained a phone number.

"Miss Zimmerman, Mr. Thompson, you have helped avoid a potentially deadly epidemic. Your government thanks you."

"You're welcome," the pair sheepishly replied simultaneously.
"As far as your gift, that information is now classified. I have your contact information. If I have need of your unique skills again I will be in touch."

"Wait a minute, you believe me?" Zoey asked in shock.

"Yes, absolutely. There are many things in this world that are unbelievable but are true. Last week would you have believed in zombie pigeons?"

"Well, no."

"Thank you again for your service today. Enjoy the ball game tonight. Goodbye."

The general gave a salute and walked off.

Standing in silent shock the pair was joined by the Diamondbacks outfielder, "You kids ready for a tour?"

"Yeah," Zoey replied still trying to take in everything that just happened.

"All right, first things first, let's stop by the team store and get you two a new jersey for the game tonight."

"Yes," Tanner shouted, "Can I get 'Tank" on the back of my jersey?"

Zoey laughed to herself, *Boys*.

Six Months Later

Zoey opened the front door and was surprised not to see someone standing there. *I know I heard the doorbell.*

She looked around but there was no one to be seen, just a large yellow envelope with a white label sitting on the front step.

She picked it up and looked at the label. There was no return address, just two words.

Zimmerman: Classified

She pulled back the tab and took out the contents; two airline tickets. One for her and one for Tanner.

Just then her cell phone rang. She flipped it open and looked at the caller ID:

Unknown Caller

She put the phone up to her ear, "Hello?"

"Agent Zimmerman, General Lucas here. Did you receive the package?"

Made in the USA
Coppell, TX
16 March 2020

16830384R00042